Belongs to:
_____

_____

THE DAY MY CLOCK BROKE

Vix Browne

By The Same Author

The Day My Monster Spoke
&
The Night My Feelings Spoke

I crafted a tale and recited it to my toddler every night for three months, At the time, we were undergoing home renovations and had limited access to books. Even a year later, my little one remained enamored with the story, prompting me to transform it into a book.

Once there was a boy who had a clock
that told him what to do and when to do it.
It let him know when to get up, and...

When to play...

When to brush his teeth

When to eat

When to go to school...

To draw...

To eat dinner...

Take a bath...

And go to bed.

Then one day his clock stopped working.

The boy woke up, LATE,
and didn't know what to do.

So, he did what he wanted.
He ate Mac and Cheese for breakfast.

Did not brush his teeth, then played, played, played, and ate more Mac and Cheese.

The boy skipped his nap and played some more.

He forgot to eat and became hangry.

Then he remembered he hadn't gone to school.
So, he grabbed his bag, found his shoes,
and ran out of the house to school.

But by the time he got to the school-School was out.

The teacher asked him, "Why are you here so late?" All his friends had gone home and he had missed them.

The boy thinks. When his toys stop
working they need new batteries.
He sees a gas station and
goes to buy batteries.

At home, the boy puts his new batteries into his clock and it works.

The boy is so happy he jumps for joy.

The next day, the boys clock told him,
"Time to wake up"

Time to wash

Time to Dress

Eat breakfast

Go to school and
see all your friends

Play...

Have dinner

Brush your teeth

And go to Bed

The boy learned that doing what you want
when you want is fun once in a while
but not all the time.

The End.

To Blake from Mom

Author

Vix was born and raised in south London. Her love for writing blossomed in 2012 when she published her first novel 'Gut Feeling' after a long struggle with dyslexia. With a great deal of determination, Victoria has not let anything hold her back.

Today, Victoria is a mom and lives in sunny California with her husband, son, and two rescue dogs, Tango and Eli.

Follow her progress on Instagram
@VixBrowneAuthor
Check out her website
www.VixBrowneAuthor.com

Made in United States
Orlando, FL
18 November 2024

54120810R00015